I Remember
Fishing
WITH DAD

I Remember

Fishing
WITH DAD

Written by
JASON DORSEY

Illustrated by
JACK DORSEY & JASON DORSEY

JUST DUST PUBLISHERS | Publishing works of redeeming value.
justdustpublishers.com

Just Dust Publishers
1025 NE Irvine Street
McMinnville OR 97128
JustDustPublishers.com

I Remember Fishing with Dad
© 2016 by Just Dust Publishers
Original art © 2015 by Jack Dorsey & Jason Dorsey
All rights reserved. Published 2016
No part of this book, neither text nor images,
may be reproduced in any manner without permission from the publisher.
To obtain consent, contact: office@JustDustPublishers.com
Printed in the United States of America
Second hardbound edition, 2016
ISBN: 978-0-9908635-6-4

Cover image: Jack Dorsey & Jason Dorsey
Cover Design: Craig Weinberg (vpdstudio.com)
Original Watercolor Art: Jack Dorsey & Jason Dorsey
Interior Design: Craig Weinberg (vpdstudio.com)

"To Dad, who took me fishing"

INTRODUCTION

My hope in *I Remember Fishing with Dad* is to show how important sacred memories are in the forming of children. Fyodor Dostoyevsky once wrote this about good memories in his classic *The Brothers Karamazov*:

> *"My dear children, perhaps you will not understand what I'm going to say to you now, for I often speak very incomprehensibly, but, I'm sure, you will remember that there's nothing higher, stronger, more wholesome and more useful in life than some good memory, especially when it goes back to the days of your childhood, to the days of your life at home. You are told a lot about your education, but some beautiful, sacred memory, preserved since, is perhaps the best education of all."*

Through story and art, I weave together the experiences I had as a boy growing up on Camano Island in the Pacific Northwest, salmon fishing with my dad--memories that shaped me into the man I am today.

It is my hope that many parents who read this book with their children will be inspired to make equally sacred memories with their children.

I remember fishing with Dad...

Jason Dorsey

Ethan crossed his arms and laid his head on the cold kitchen counter. He blinked as he watched his dad spread peanut butter across a piece of bread, preparing their lunches for the day.

He was not used to getting up when it was still dark. And even though he was dressed and ready to go, he was sleepy.

The Fishing Hole

Port Susan

Saratoga Passage

Road to the State Park

The State Park

Our House

"Ethan, go splash some water on your face," his dad said. "It will help you wake up."

Ethan was excited and a little bit nervous to go fishing with his father. They were staying on the very island where his dad grew up, and where his dad had fished with Ethan's grandfather when he was just a boy, too.

Ethan's dad drove the old family truck and a trailer that carried their boat. They arrived at the state park on Camano Island just as the sunlight began to break over the horizon.

After Ethan's dad backed the trailer down the boat ramp, he told Ethan, "I need you to hold the rope so the boat doesn't float away when I push it off the trailer."

Ethan didn't want to disappoint his dad, and he especially didn't want to lose the boat. He held the rope tight as the boat glided into the water.

Once aboard, his dad started the motor and turned on the boat's lights. "Why do we need lights?" Ethan asked.

"So the other boats can see us," he said, and revved up the engine. "Keep your eyes open for driftwood. If we run into a log, it would be bad for the boat." Ethan nodded and took his post to watch.

Ethan's dad piloted the boat to a spot that he promised was the best fishing hole. He showed Ethan how to prepare his line to catch salmon. His dad hooked a weight onto the line, then he attached a flasher to the weight. Finally he tied a leader with hooks to the flasher. The bait they used was little fish called herring.

Herring

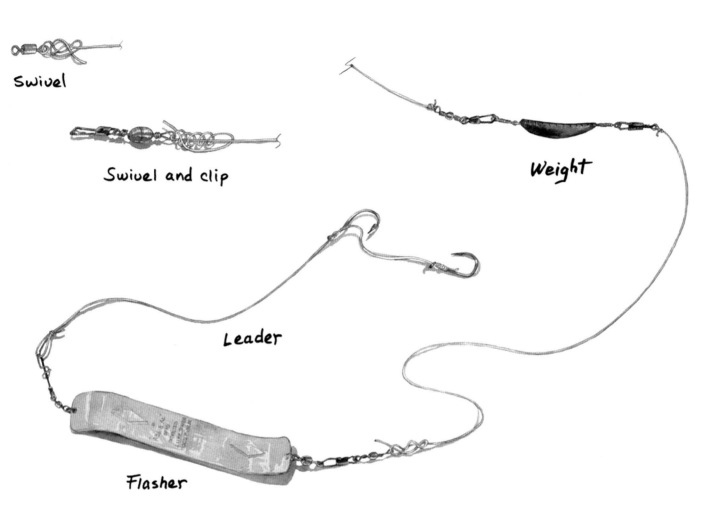

Swivel

Swivel and clip

Weight

Leader

Flasher

Ethan could hardly wait for his dad to finish. Finally, he said he was done! He showed Ethan how to slowly lower his line with the weight, flasher, and herring into the water.

Then they waited.

Ethan watched seagulls circle overhead.

They dove, trying to catch some herring.

Ethan yawned and waited. And waited.

"It's a lot of waiting, isn't it?" asked his dad.

Ethan nodded.

"I remember fishing with my dad," said Ethan's dad. "When I was just about your age, he and I had one of the most exciting times of my life." His dad shook his head and smiled. "I don't think there is a much better feeling than hooking a big salmon, but the best part of fishing was just being with Dad."

"Tell me about it," said Ethan, "the exciting time."

"Well," he said, "one Friday after school the bus dropped me off and I ran as fast as I could into the house."

Dad chuckled, "Looks like someone's excited." Dad was excited too. We were going to fish at the annual Salmon Derby the next morning. "I hope we win this year!" I said as I gulped down my cookies and milk.

That night, I dreamed of salmon, seagulls, and winning the derby with Dad.

Early the next morning, while it was still dark, Dad opened my bedroom door and whispered.

"Son, it's time to get up if we want to be the first boat on the water."

I stumbled to the bathroom and splashed cold water on my face to help me wake up. Then I pulled on my lucky fishing hat and ran outside to check how windy it was.

The trees were still.

s we drove down the hill to the boat ramp,
ne water below was as smooth as glass.

's a perfect fishing day," said Dad.

19

"Dad, we're the first ones to the boat ramp!" I said.

Dad's eyes gleamed. "Maybe this is our year to win. The big salmon are caught early in the morning."

Dad pushed our boat off the trailer, and I gripped the rope.

21

As we pushed away from shore, we saw the lights of another truck headed to the boat launch.

"Hurry, Dad! Start the motor!"

Dad turned the key. Nothing.

He tried again.

Still nothing.

The other boat was in the water now. It was our neighbor, old Mr. Anderson, and his new boat named *Trophy*.

"For crying out loud!" Dad muttered. His smile was gone. "This old engine acts up at the worst time."

As Dad tinkered with the engine, I watched boat after boat launch and race off to catch the early salmon.

Finally, the old engine roared to life.

"I hope there are some fish left for us!" Dad shouted over the wind as we raced to our favorite fishing hole.

I hope so, too, I thought as the cold spray hit my face. *One for Dad and one for me.*

As we came around the point, I saw fishermen already at our fishing hole, trolling for salmon.

27

Seagulls were there too, circling and diving for herring.

"The big king salmon are chasing those herring," Dad said.

I was afraid we were too late and had missed the bite. "Bite" is the best time to catch salmon, when they are feeding.

Dad rigged my line.

"Hurry, Dad, hurry!" I could hardly wait for him to finish.

"Be patient, son. You won't catch anything without this herring!" After what seemed like forever, Dad finished.

I let my weight, flasher, and herring down into the water. I sat back in my chair and waited for a salmon to bite. I watched as the morning colors danced on the waves that rocked our boat. I watched my pole bob up and down to the rhythm of the flasher.

I watched drips of water fall from Dad's nose. I smiled and thought, *Dad's nose always drips when it is cold.*

31

As we passed the *Trophy,* Dad said, "Look. Old Mr. Anderson has a big one." I looked up just in time to see Mr. Anderson net a big king salmon. *I wish Dad had caught that salmon,* I thought.

Boats trolled back and forth. Suddenly, my pole jerked toward the water.

"I had a strike!" I shouted.

I yanked my pole from the pole holder and felt the tug of a salmon.

"Keep your pole tip up!" Dad reminded me.

The salmon jumped in the distance. It took all of my strength to keep the pole tip up. My arms ached, my hands shook, but I kept reeling the salmon toward the boat. When it was close enough, Dad netted it.

"Way to go, son!" Dad slapped me on the back. "That's a good fish." But I knew it wasn't big enough to win a prize at the Derby.

It's your turn now, Dad, I thought.

Back and forth, back and forth we trolled. I watched the yellows and pinks of morning become the blues and greens of midday.

I watched the other boats motor off to try their luck somewhere else.

The afternoon sun beat down on us. I knew time was running out. The derby would be over in less than an hour. All the fishermen would be weighing their salmon.

"Son, it's time we went home," Dad said. "We need to go weigh your fish."

"Please, Dad," I begged. "Don't give up yet. Just one last try?"

Dad looked at me and smiled. "Sure. One more try.""

With fresh herring on our hooks, we let our lines down. The sun warmed my body. I closed my eyes and dozed and dreamed about catching a big king salmon.

"Fish On!"

Dad's yell woke me.

"It's a big one!"

I stared as Dad's pole tip bent to the water. The line whizzed off the reel as the salmon dove. Dad wrenched the pole tip up, and inch by inch, wrestled the salmon toward the boat.

My hands shook as I lowered the net into the water. I held it still.

"Here it comes. Here it comes," Dad whispered.

The salmon's silver side flashed. I lifted the net high. The salmon was in it.

We had caught our king salmon!

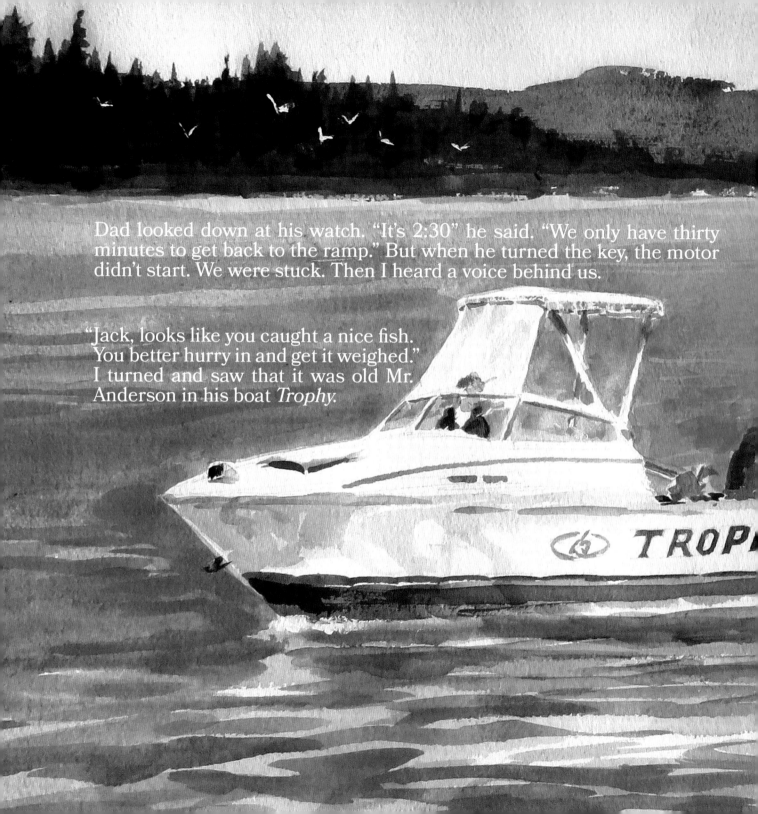

Dad looked down at his watch. "It's 2:30" he said. "We only have thirty minutes to get back to the ramp." But when he turned the key, the motor didn't start. We were stuck. Then I heard a voice behind us.

"Jack, looks like you caught a nice fish. You better hurry in and get it weighed." I turned and saw that it was old Mr. Anderson in his boat *Trophy*.

Dad said, "This motor is broken.
I can't go anywhere."

Mr. Anderson looked at his watch. Then he said, "Catch
this rope. I'll give you a tow."

And he did. He pulled us to the boat ramp.

The last fishermen were weighing their fish. We had arrived just in time. My heart pounded as we walked through the crowd. I proudly hoisted my salmon on the scales. It weighed 5 pounds.

Next, Dad heaved his fish onto the scale. I watched the scale sink. I knew it was one of the biggest caught that day—but would it be a winner?

Looking down at me, Dad smiled. "I'm glad we put our lines down that one last time."

The judges finished weighing all the fish. They put away the scales. The fishermen waited for the judges to announce the winners.

Seagulls circled overhead. I kicked at pebbles underneath my feet.

Finally, the judges called out the winners.

Dad didn't win first place.

But he did win second! And he asked if I could stand next to him for the picture. We made the headline of our local newspaper, and Dad used the $500 he won to help buy a new motor for the boat.

"I remember fishing with Dad...and I still think that there's hardly anything better than a calm morning when you can watch the colors dance on the waves, when you can hold a fishing pole in your hands and hear the cry of the gulls, and, most of all, when you can be with your dad."

Stanwood NEWS

Stanwood, Snohomish County, Wash. 98292   SEVENTY-THIRD YEAR   September 14, 1977   No. 11

Dick's $1,000 fish story

SALMON DERBY WINNERS—Dick Anderson, left, of Camano Island, won the $1000 first prize in the annual Salmon Derby last Sunday, with a 26 pound, 8 ounce King Salmon caught Saturday. Second prize went to Jack Dorsey, also of Camano Island, with a 10 pound, four and one-half ounce fish caught Sunday. Jason Dorsey eyes the $500 fish. Third winner, not pictured, was Art Schroeder of Marysville, who caught a 10 pound, one ounce fish Saturday, for the $100 prize. Anderson, who said that the day of the "big fish" was also the Anderson's 33rd wedding anniversary, caught his winner off Rocky Point by fishing shallow, using squid with a little herring stripped in, and almost lost it when the leader broke as it was going in the net. Saturday's total fish catch was 45, with 40 being entered on Sunday.

—NEWSphoto by Howard Hansen

Ethan and his dad sat silently for a while. Suddenly Ethan's rod lunged forward, almost snapping from his hands. Ethan grasped it as if it were the most precious possession he would ever own.

He yelled, **"Fish On!"**

His dad scrambled for the net.

It was then Ethan knew that his father was right.
There is hardly anything better than being with your dad.

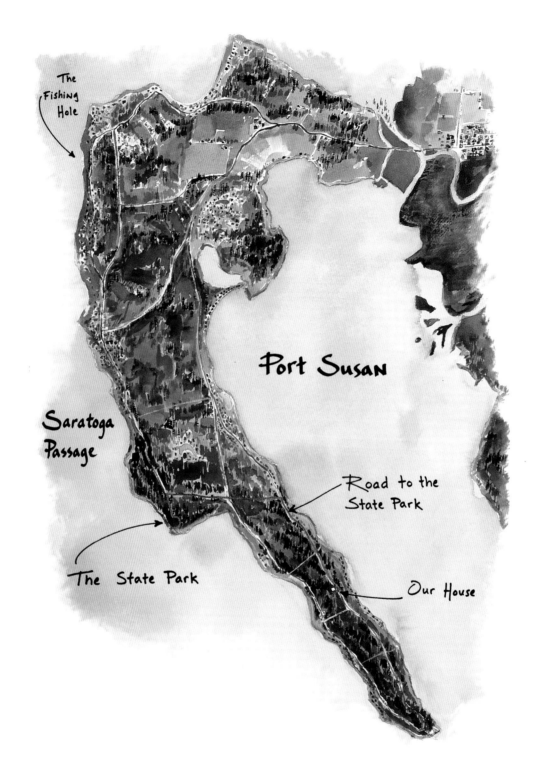

The Fishing Hole

Port Susan

Saratoga Passage

Road to the State Park

The State Park

Our House

ACKNOWLEDGMENTS

I would like to thank my friends: Matt Hale, who helped me develop an early draft of this book; Paul Baumgarten, who took the photographs for it; and David Lichty, who encouraged me to create more dramatic tension in the story.

Esther Heshenhorn was a great coach as I tried to figure out the ins and outs of writing children's books.

And I am especially thankful for Shelley Houston, who is helping me bring this decade old project to light.

–Jason Dorsey

To learn more about Jason's passion to share the beauty of Camano Island, Washington with the world, check out his blog at www.sunnyshorestudio.wordpress.com.

Jason and Jack Dorsey - January 2015

Jason now serves as a Presbyterian pastor in Redmond, Washington, near his father and mother.
They all enjoy painting, and occasionally Jack and Jason still go fishing together.